BLACK WOOLLY PONY, WHITE CHALK HORSE

In this book there are two country stories. *Bridget and William*, the story of a girl and her pony, is set in Yorkshire, where Jane Gardam grew up and still has a house today. *Horse* tells of a girl's efforts to save an ancient landmark that is under threat of being destroyed – as, indeed, is the real chalk horse, which is situated above Kilburn on the Hambleton Hills.

Jane Gardam has twice won the Whitbread Award – for her children's book *The Hollow Land* and, in 1991, for her adult novel *The Queen of the Tambourine*. In addition, *God on the Rocks* was runner-up for the Booker Prize and *Bridget and William* was Commended for the Carnegie Medal. Her other titles include *The Summer After the Funeral*, *Through the Dolls' House Door* and *A Few Fair Days*.

To Bridget
(Bridget and William)

To Susan
(Horse)

First published 1981 as *Bridget and William*
and 1982 as *Horse* by Julia MacRae Books

This edition published 1993 by
Walker Books Ltd, 87 Vauxhall Walk
London SE11 5HJ

4 6 8 10 9 7 5 3

Printed and bound in England

British Library Cataloguing in Publication Data
A catalogue record for this book is
available from the British Library.
ISBN 0-7445-2226-9

Black Woolly Pony, White Chalk Horse

JANE GARDAM

Illustrated by
Janet Rawlins

WALKER BOOKS
LONDON

CONTENTS

Bridget & William

Chapter 1

When Bridget was seven she moved to a new farm over in the next dale, and very high.

"Now, face it," Old Todd said to her father, looking round at the heather and the wild sky above it, "It's a grand spot, but it's high. You'll be snowed in maybe once or twice in a winter. It'll do for sheep but it's no place for milk cattle and if you keep a horse it'll have to stand int' stable three parts of the year."

"No horses," said Bridget's father, "One horse eats like five sheep. No profit. No sense in a horse."

"Not a horse for Bridget?" asked Old Todd, "And three grand stables lying empty? Not much else for a little lass up here, high as this."

"Horses is only for townsfolks now," said Bridget's father.

Bridget looked down from the yard gate she was sitting on. The road wound away, down out of

sight, into the trees on the one-in-three hill and into the beck. You couldn't see the beck from High Farm but you could hear it rushing. Then you could see the track come out again beyond the beck and wind away and away over the moors.

Far to either side of it there was a dot here and a dot there—low farms with smoke rising. Purple heather came rolling in to the dale bottoms to the sharp edges of bright green fields—squares and oblongs and strips and one field the shape of a boot. Then the track disappeared over a brow near the Saxon Cross and even beyond that you could not see the village. Just a bluebell haze and white clouds hurtling. There were seven white gates along this lovely road. Bridget imagined a horse trotting.

"Think of opening and shutting that lot of gates, coming home of a dark night," said Bridget's mother.

"Council might put in cattle grids," said her father.

"That it might not," said Old Todd, "Cattle grids cost thousands. They'll put in no cattle grids for one high farm. Long gates is best anyways. For horses. All ways over."

"We're having no horses," said Bridget's father. "If Bridget gets lonely I'll buy her a lamb. Maybe two. Then next summer she can sell them and buy four. Learn some farming. Mind, we've not bought this farm yet. It's high. We're still only talking."

"I'd *like* a horse," said Bridget.

"We're having no horse," said her father.

Chapter 2

But when they moved to High Farm there came a letter with a cheque in it from Bridget's town auntie: and Bridget saw it before anybody else because the postman gave her a shout from over beyond Muirs.

"Here you *youths*," he shouted.

Bridget was with two other girls walking to the school bus down the long track. It was a dark morning and sleeting. The postman had tooted from out of the dark, hearing their voices. He had been listening out for Bridget because his van hadn't felt like swimming the beck or climbing the one-in-three hill to High Farm that morning. There were stories about long-ago people and ponies and traps and even sheep who had toppled over the edge of Bridget's one-in-three hill and down into Black Hole Pot below. The hill was supposed to be haunted. Bridget had to think of very cheerful and sensible things when she walked the hill in the dark.

During term-time in winter she

walked down in the morning dark and back in the afternoon dark and never saw High Farm at all—only its lights saying goodbye as she left it and waiting for her again when she got home. "Might as well live in Finland and have done," said the town auntie, "Half the year in the dark and half of that under snow. Trolls and hedgehogs!" Bridget's aunt had moved down to London when she was young. "What a place to grow up on. *Moors*," she said. "Thank goodness I got away anyway." But she was always on the telephone.

"Letter for Bridget," shouted the postman. "Think on now. Look alive. D'you want a lift in?"

Bridget and Susan and Adrienne from over Esklетts sat in a bunch in the post van. Susan and Adrienne were sisters from a lower-down farm and Bridget caught them up and walked with them the long road to the bus nearly every day. But Susan and Adrienne mostly talked to each other, being very like twins.

"Three letters for Bridget," said the postman, "Hello then—it's a birthday."

"There's things for your father, too," he said, "But bills mainly and *Farmer's Weekly*. Put them int' bin, Bridget, up by the last gate when you get out, and take them up on with you when you go home tonight."

"*Is't* thy birthday?" asked Adrienne.

"Aye," said Bridget.

"Happy-returns-and-what-did-you-get?"

"Dad give me a sheep and Mum give me a hair-brush."

"What's in your letters?"

"Cards from both Grans and one

from my London auntie. With a pink form in it."

"Pink form?" said Susan.

"Let's look at it," said the postman stopping at the third gate. Bridget got out, holding the auntie's letter. It was her gate, the third one, for they took turns. She did not give the pink form to the postman but let it flap in her hand. She dragged the heavy gate open and then shut it

again when the van was through. She climbed back in.

"I'd think it was money," she said. Susan looked at it. "Yes it's money," she said, "That's a cheque. It's terrible writing. It's done in a hurry."

"That'll be London," said the postman.

"Is that one nothing or two nothings?" asked Bridget.

Adrienne grabbed the cheque and sounded very solemn. "It's two nothings," she said, "It's *two* nothings."

The postman at the fourth gate borrowed the cheque. "It's two nothings all right," he said. "Wait

on. There's a message ont' card. I'll read it next gate."

But the next gate had snow up against it worse than he'd found coming and they all had to get out; and the next gate had cold cows leaning against it, not inclined to move over, and everyone had to get out again. The seventh gate was

Bridget's gate again and she gave the postman the message to read while she did the opening and shutting. When she got back in the van the postman said, "The message reads it's for buying an 'orse. For not owt but an 'orse. Or to send it back."

Bridget left her two grannies' cards with her father's post in the bin by the Saxon Cross, but the auntie's message and the pink form she kept under her jersey and tee-shirt next to her skin all day.

Chapter 3

"And she'll just fall off it," said Bridget's mother at tea-time, "And give me one more thing to worry over. Just think on—flying over the edge of the one-in-three. Whirling washed away down the beck in flood. Head over heels. This isn't London. Parks and soft acres. This is *moors*."

Bridget sat not speaking. Quiet and still.

"We'd best send back this cheque," said her father, eating birthday cake. Bridget grew quieter and stiller.

But he was joking.

Everyone had another slice. Everyone thought about it. A horse.

"Special clothes next, I suppose,"

said her mother, "Let alone the cost of its keep. Riding clothes. Hard black hats."

But Bridget's mother liked clothes and she had begun to look sparkly. Bridget said clothes didn't matter.

"Any extra from this cheque," said her father, "Anything extra in the neighbourhood of this horse—let me tell you—goes on riding *lessons*, not riding *clothes*. We'll have no broken necks."

"And wherever riding lessons?" said her mother, "Round here?"

"We'll find some. That's a detail. We have to have a cheap, safe horse first."

Which was why William arrived.

He appeared with Old Todd round the bend of the one-in-three a splashy spring day, and at first you only saw the tops of their two heads coming. Old Todd had heard tell of the pony over Pickering way. It had been on another cold farm, high on a moor. His owner had grown to be twelve and large and out of him. He was rough as heather, black as a tarn and round as a partridge. He looked at Bridget as Todd brought him right up to her on the farm step. "Name of William," said Todd. William pushed his rough head at her. Then he lifted his top lip and began to eat her coat collar.

"Savage," said her father, "All savage, horses. Scare me daylights. He can't see out of his eyes. He's like an ape. He needs his hair cut."

"He's just woolly," said Bridget, "He smells grand."

The pony stopped eating her coat collar and put his nose under her ear and blew warm air round the back of her neck. It was hot and tickly and sounded like a slow motor-bike. “Hey, give over,” said Bridget and the pony gave over. Right from the beginning it did most things Bridget said.

He didn’t do everything Todd said though, or anything Bridget’s father said. He had what Todd called “a will to ’im”. “Not a baddun, mind,” said Todd. “I hear tell he’s not a baddun. Likes youths. But he has a will. Rather the rovin’ kind. Likes rovin’ the country round. Not unlike this youth here.”

Bridget said she wasn’t a youth she was a lass.

Old Todd said, “Youth is the old word for any young.”

By the time winter came round again William was as much a part of High Farm as the sheep and the sheep-dogs and the ten Galloway cows and the barn owl who sat thinking in the angle of the new barn, and you could not imagine life without him. Bridget had learned to ride him at a riding school twelve miles away where all the riders wore smart clothes and sat very straight on ponies that shone like conkers. They didn't at all understand Bridget in her tee-shirt and jeans and they gasped with horror at William. Even their ponies gasped and juddered away from him as he bounced up, swinging his tail.

“That’s no pony. It’s a mammoth. A baby mammoth,” said someone and everyone laughed. But Bridget didn’t mind. William was her friend and they weren’t. She had eight lessons and that was all. Old Todd said that she'd do nicely now. "I can scarce believe *that*," said her mother who had begun to read pony books. Bridget's mother had taken to going to talk to William on cold days, in the stable while Bridget was at school, and when winter came and the water froze in his trough she was always running out to break the ice. When it got really cold in February Bridget's mother began to run with blankets.

"That William'll be int' sitting room next," said Bridget's father. "Ask me, he's more trouble than enough. Bridget can't ride him this weather. Whenever it stops snowing and one-in-three's clear for him, like as not she's at school. We can't ride him. He's fat as a pork pie. He looks like a pork pie. He'd be more *use* as a pork pie."

"I thought," said Bridget's mother, "Maybe I'd learn. After our new baby's come. Learn to ride."

"We'll get the baby here first," said Bridget's father. "One event at a time."

Chapter 4

It was a long winter. The price of feed went higher and the weather grew worse. "It'd be a good deal of sense to sell that William," said Bridget's father, "and buy another when summer comes. He just stands there eating. If we've a bad lambing time and nothing to sell there'll be no ways to it. He'll have to go if we lose lambs."

Bridget prayed for a good lambing time, but nobody seemed to hear. The weather turned from black frost to snow to black frost again. The one-in-three was too dangerous for even the tractor and Bridget couldn't get through to school. The post van only sometimes got through as far as the beck and the postman tooted for Bridget in vain. Lambs were born in blizzards and died in the snow before they had drawn breath and Bridget's father was out all night looking for them. The kitchen was full of bleating draggly lambs. Bridget and her mother spent hours with feeding bottles, but still a great many died.

One night there was the most tremendous storm of all and new snow swept up the side of the farmhouse to the bedroom windows and the wind screamed all night long. Nobody got to sleep till morning. When they did wake up, the day felt quite late. The wind had gone and there was a very queer silence. Bridget scratching at the ice on the inside of her windowpane, looked out at rolling soft white seas.

The fields had gone. The track had gone down the dale. The seven gates had gone. The sun was shining all over the white ocean. "We're like Ararat," said Bridget, "The ark has landed. I'd better go see William."

She was stroking William after breaking his ice and giving him some feed when her father came in to the stable and stood looking at her.

"Did you go to bed?" said Bridget, "Have you seen—? Everything's disappeared. Isn't it still?"

Her father stood frowning. Then he said, "Bridget, the telephone's down. If I walk beside you down the one-in-three slowly and put you on the way, do you think you could follow the track to the village? On William?"

They set off down the hill and it was terrible. Bridget loved it. Carefully she watched where William cleverly put his feet. She walked to one side of him, her

father, not too happily on the other. At the bottom of the hill there was no beck. You could not even see the hand-rail of the little bridge. But through the wood it seemed better. The snow was hard-packed under the new fall. They could see signs of the first gate showing ahead. "I have to get back quick now," said her father. "Now just go steadily on till you get to the village and get the doctor. You'll be all right on William. The gates'll guide you. You'll like as not be able to step across them if there's any not been left open, which I doubt. Tell him to try and get as far as he can in his land-rover."

"What shall I say?"

"Say the baby's thinking of arriving early."

"Never!" said Bridget. "Silly thing. Silly as lambs."

Chapter 5

Up on his back she said, "Now then William," and he stood quite still and thoughtful for a moment. Then he gave his head a shake and set off. First he put down his hooves carefully. When he found that they didn't slip about he gave his head another shake—a rather jolly shake—and began to step springily.

After the first gate he gave his tail a wave and went merrily on. The snow began to get rather deep and soft and Bridget's stomach began to go squirmy. They went safely, tappy-lappy, through the second gate and along the shallow lane. And through the third gate. And through the fourth gate. And over the hill and down the deep dip. And there William stopped—stopped right in front of a nice smooth sweep of snow like the slope of a tent-side, no mark on it but the pricked out stars of a bird's feet. "Git on," said Bridget. William shook his head and made the motor-bike noise. "Git on."

But he wouldn't. Bridget remembered what old Todd had once said, "William'll know," (her mother had been worrying about her being out on the empty moor alone). "If there's danger the horse knows more than the rider. Let her give him his head and she'll be grand."

"All right then, William," she said, "Do what you want," and she let the reins go slack.

William turned carefully aside

and tiptoed very slowly away from the road and up the bank, high up along where the wall must be. Bridget closed her eyes—tighter when William stumbled—but after a minute he shook his head again

and was down and walking springily. The fifth gate was nothing. The sixth gate had disappeared so it was no trouble. Everything looked like somewhere new and the old track—which was just the hint of a delve in the fields—wound on. And on. And on. Bridget began to wonder if she had gone through six gates or only five? Or only four? She looked for landmarks and there were none. She looked over her shoulder and up to where High Farm stood and was surprised to find it had gone, too. Snow was coming again. Already it began to spit in her face.

William plodded on—rather solemnly now. Still there was no last gate, no Saxon Cross and all of a sudden Bridget was afraid. The same moment she felt afraid William stumbled and stopped.

Then she remembered Old Todd again. "A horse will only lose its nerve when the rider does," and she wiped her face and sat straight and gripped William hard with her knees. "Oh come on you soft thing," she said. "I thought horses were supposed to love snow. Move on now." And William plunged on and at the next bend he made the motor-bike noise, because there was the seventh gate—two black post tops and the Saxon Cross beyond them. Beyond the cross the road was like icing sugar, still shiny before it dries and it had sprays of safe black grit thrown about it all the way in to the village.

Chapter 6

"Our baby's coming," she told the doctor. He had just got his land-rover started outside the house and looked as though it had been quite a battle. It was a wonderful machine that knew the country almost as well as William, and Bridget was pleased to see both it and the doctor. She was scarlet-faced. Her back was soaking with snow and there was ice all over her front.

"You never got through from up there! On that horse!"

"It wasn't that bad," said Bridget, "Matter of fact it was grand." William tossed his tail about. His tail was sopped and his mane was frosty.

"Well put that gorilla in my stable and get in the car with me. Or better still, stay down here till I get back. They'll see to you both." The land-rover sputtered off in clouds of blue smoke. "I'll maybe walk the last bit," he said, "You

get inside the house and keep warm."

But Bridget didn't. She stamped about a bit and gave William some sugar. Then she set off back with him again, finding it easier in the doctor's tracks, like good King

Wenceslas. "Good William," she said.

When she reached the sloping smooth place where William had refused to step, there was the doctor's car looking extremely upset, sunk down up to its windows. She slid off William's back up along the wall again and down, and then followed in the doctor's footprints which were already nearly full up with more snow. Her face stung. She got in under William's wet plump flank and tried—on the one-in-three at last—to think cheerfully about cheerful things. But it was a bit hard. The hill was dreadful and dark. The sleet stung. A bad lambing, she thought, no sign of Spring, no feed for William. Nothing to look forward to.

But then she saw the lights of the house shining and she was home. And as she stopped to get at the stable door she heard a noise like a lamb from the house. It was a noisy bleat. Mum's even got them in the bedrooms now, she thought —and remembered the baby!

It seemed awful to have forgotten him. She found she was very, very excited—and blushing. "I'll never tell it," she thought, "That I forgot."

Her father came in to the stable. He was very red and strong-looking and didn't seem tired at all. "This lamb's going to live," he said, "A boy lamb. Grand and

strong and noisy. The doctor got here just in time." He put his arm round Bridget—and then he put his other arm on tired William!

"We won't be getting rid of him? William?" said Bridget. "Will we? Not now? I couldn't have done it just walking."

"Not never," said her father, "Not never. Now come and get warm and see this new youth. Then we'll get William warm. And tomorrow we'll sit down and write all about it to that poor town auntie."

HORSE

Chapter 1

Susan lived at Sandy Top. It was a farm on the top of the Hartington Hills.

To get to school she could run down the hill to the road and round in a semi-circle to the village square. Or she could run a little way down the hill and branch off down Sandy Back, a zig-zaggy, rosy, brambly lane, very narrow. Or she could climb up behind the farm and run down the steep slope on the other side.

If she went the semi-circle way along the road it took half an hour. If she went the zig-zaggy way between the brambles it took nearly half an hour. But if she went the steep harum-scarum way down the slope she was at school in two minutes. If she had been a hawk or a smallish eagle she could have been there in half a minute by diving down the school chimney pot which was directly below her, round like the tops of the heads of the other children running about like marbles in the village square.

But there was another reason why Susan liked going to school down the steep slope. It meant that she could run across a horse.

Not round a horse.

Not away from a horse.

Not on the back of a horse.

But across a horse.

The horse was utterly huge. It was a thousand times bigger than Susan and twenty people could sit in its eye. It lay all across the great slope, one foot prettily lifted and its head gently drooped and its tail flowing free. A very pleasant, well-behaved sort of horse, though of course you couldn't actually see what it was as you ran across it, only when you looked back at it from the stile that jumped you into the village square.

Horse was a cut out. A great big drawing that looked as if it had been cut round with giant's scissors, and it had shone very white in the green grass when it had been finished off two hundred years ago because it had had six tons of white lime spread over it.

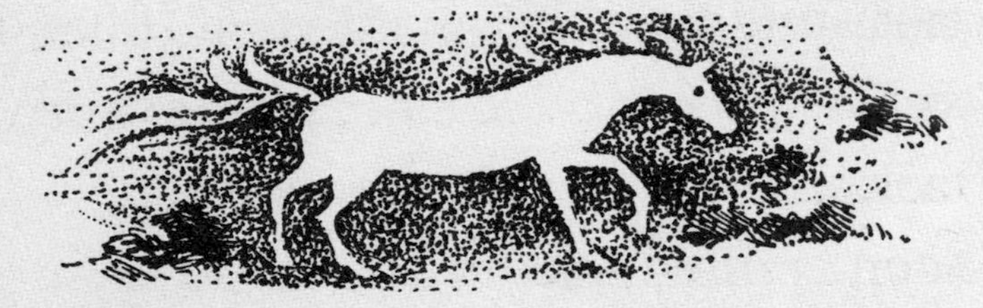

'Horse' he was always called. Not 'The Horse' or 'The White Horse' like other ones are called in other parts of England. This horse had nothing special about him. He wasn't mixed up with legends or History. Mr. Grandly at the pub could even remember his father telling about when he had been made. Nobody came fussing to photograph him any more or write boring books about him. He was just a member of the village. Just Horse. And beautiful.

When Susan first went to school her mother took her down the slope as far as Horse's hoof. Soon her mother only took her as far as Horse's middle. Soon again she only took her to Horse's mane, always waiting for her to turn at the stile and wave. At the end of two terms Susan's mother said goodbye from the kitchen and Susan went up and over and down Horse all by herself—though she still found she turned when she got to the stile and waved. This was partly out of habit and partly because it seemed unfriendly to Horse if she didn't.

And she did this for ages—until she was nearly seven.

Then one day in a wet summer Susan turned to wave to Horse as usual but slipped from the stile and fell in the mud. The school teacher, Mrs. Pail, was a fuss-pot about mud, and quite rightly because she not only taught the children, she gave them their dinner and cleaned the school as well. She was a wonderful teacher and Pure Gold was Mrs. Pail, and when

stuffy people said that she *lowered* herself by all this extra work she swept them out of the school on the end of her squeezy mop. She sometimes swept

the children out too when they were muddy, and made them learn their sums in the street on Mr. Grandly's bench. Mr. Grandly kept the door of his pub always wide open in order to miss nothing. He hated children. They needed watching, he said.

So Susan tried to get the mud off. She rubbed at her skirt and her sock and her leg. The rain pattered down above her head in the leaves of the rowan tree which had a wire basket fastened to it for Mr. Grandly's morning paper to be delivered. Mr. Grandly was one hundred years old and he didn't step far afield, not even to the Shop.

"No wave today then?"

Susan jumped.

Mr. Grandly was tall as a silo, under the rowan tree sheltering from the rain. If there was nothing odd about dear old Horse who was two hundred years old, there was plenty to give you the shivers in Mr. Grandly. He stared far out in front of him with his pale, hundred-year-old eyes. He could see things far away. He could see a hare on a ridge or a sheep in a fence or a lark in the air. They say that the older Mr. Grandly got the further away he could see.

"No wave at Horse today?"

Susan blushed and felt silly. She thought, I won't wave at Horse again.

"About time."

Susan looked up then, cross. "About time what?"

"About time to stop."

"Why?" she said, fierce.

"Why? Because he's scarce there. Scarce there to wave at."

"Susan will you come in this minute," called Mrs. Pail from the school step. "What's two drops of rain to be sheltering under trees?"

Susan ran across the square.

"And whatever's all this mud?" Mrs. Pail tutted and flurried her inside. Susan forgot about Horse then until home time.

But then, climbing back over the stile, she remembered.

Scarce there to wave at.

She looked at the slope above her—it was still raining—and she saw that Horse was not sparkling white in the green grass. Not any more.

And he was going all woolly round the edges.

His nose seemed to be buried in a bramble bush. His body seemed to be decorated all over with dandelion clumps. His floaty tail you could hardly see for bilberries and tough black ling. How long has this been going on? she thought. Rain streamed down Horse leaving quite deep channels, spoiling his shape.

Susan thought, It's ages and ages and ages since I really looked at Horse.

Chapter 2

The next day she ran down to school early and looked in at Mr. Grandly's open door. He had taken his newspaper already this morning and lay stretched out on a very long wooden sofa in his bar. There was nothing else in his bar except a huge fireplace and two or three ancient chairs on his flat-stoned floor. Several old photographs of Horse hung above a table in the corner where the bottles stood. Horse in the photographs looked sharp as a horse of glass or steel. He looked pressed out of the grass by a huge pastry cutter. Dazzling white.

Susan looked.

"Get on to school," said Mr. Grandly from behind his newspaper, "I can't do with bairns."

"It was Horse."

"Bairns and attachments."

"I haven't got attachments," said Susan. "What's attachments?"

"What bairns faffs their time on," said Mr. Grandly. "Hoops and kites. It was hoops and kites first. Followed by crashing dolly-carts. Followed by scooters. Followed by bikes, from penny-farthings on. Then it was skates—roller skates and skate boards. For eighty years across this square, I've been warring with bairns and attachments."

"I'm by myself."

"Catapults, arrows, darts."

"I've got none."

"It was hoops and kites to blame for First World War," said Mr. Grandly. "It was roller-skates responsible for Second. Then came the skate boards and so I dare say there's to be Third. Too much pleasure, that's what bairns get."

"I think you're silly," said Susan and Mr. Grandly lowered the paper and showed his terrible pale eyes.

"I want to say about Horse."

"What about Horse?"

"It's going away. It's fading out."

Mr. Grandly lifted the paper back up again. "I know that," he said.

Susan went away.

"Have you looked at Horse?" Susan asked her mother. "He's gone all woolly."

"Oh, it's just the rain. It makes the weeds grow."

"No. He's different. He's all moth-eaten looking. You can hardly make him out."

"Well this is a third bad summer."

"Can't we do something about him?"

"Well I dare say we shall," said her mother, "one of these days, likely."

"Horse is looking awful," said Susan to Mrs. Pail.

"Go on with your History, Susan."

"But Horse is looking awful. He's fading out. He's all over bilberries and weeds."

"We'll go up there for Nature," said Mrs. Pail, "when it fairs up."

In the Shop Susan said to the Post Lady, "It's so wet Horse is fading out."

The people in the Shop laughed and someone gave Susan a sweet. "You're right old-fashioned," said the Post Lady. "Horse won't fade out. He'll be

there after all of us, as he was here before."

"They say," said Susan to Mr. Grandly putting her head round his door, "that Horse will last us all out."

"Who say?"

"My mother and Mrs. Pail and the Shop."

"They keep their eyes shut," said Mr. Grandly opening his wide so that Susan hurried away.

Then she went to see the wood carver. He was Mr. Grandly's son and he carved beautiful tables and chairs and sent them all over the world. He had made the village quite famous though his customers never actually came into the village because he lived outside it, a mile round towards Susan's side of the hill. The wood carver didn't come in to the village either in case he met his father. He didn't speak to his father. There had been some old quarrel.

Susan decided she would take the long way round home. She called in at the wood carver's shop and sniffed up the lovely smell of wood-shavings.

"Have some ringlets," said young Mr. Grandly who was seventy-five and very jolly, "to hang in your bonny brown hair." He scattered cork-screw curls of wood shavings all over Susan's head.

"Horse is fading out," said Susan.

"Who sez?"

"I've seen. I run on it. Every day. Twice."

"Well I never," said young Mr. Grandly, "you're wearing it out that's what it is, Susan. I dare say it'll pull itself together with winter and a good frost."

"It looks awful."

"I've not seen it in years to tell the truth," said young Mr Grandly. "It's like the back of your hand—you don't look."

"That's what your father said."

"Is it then," said the wood carver turning back to smoothing the wing of an angel for a church pew.

Chapter 3

Hardly a fortnight later, on a sunny dry day and the whole school—all thirty of them—tearing about for play-time in the village square, there was a noise like an earthquake coming, or a tank regiment. It went on, louder and louder, nearer and nearer and in to the square burst a huge lorry with a trailer yoked up to its back as long as the village street. The trailer was piled high with gigantic pipes all lashed loosely together with wires. The clatter was frightful.

All the children rushed for cover. Mrs. Pail came to the school door red in the face waving a drying-up cloth.

Mr Grandly appeared in his porch like a large dark statue.

The great lorry came to rest shuddering horribly in the middle of the little square and the driver, high above everybody's head, sat examining a dirty piece of paper in his cab.

"Sandy Top, Grandpa?" he asked.

Mr Grandly turned on his heel and shut his door.

"Sandy Top? Sandy Back?" he asked Mrs. Pail.

"What about Sandy Top and Sandy Back?"

"Delivery of drain pipes."

"*Drain* pipes?"

"That's it. Forestry."

"*Forestry*?"

"That's right. Government. Planting trees."

"We don't have trees here," said Mrs. Pail. "They don't grow here saving the odd rowan and the hedge trees and the hawthorns."

"You're going to have," said the man, "thousands of them. Christmas trees."

"Where?"

"Up yonder," said the driver. "Over yon scratty bank. They're starting digging any day. Maybe this week. I've been rushed over. Ahead with the drain pipes."

"But what about Horse?" asked Mrs. Pail.

The driver looked at the broad, tangly hill-side.

"What horse?" he said.

"They can't. They mustn't. They won't," cried Susan bursting in on young Mr. Grandly on her way home. Today she could not bear to run across Horse.

Young Mr. Grandly put down his adze and looked long and hard at her as she told the tale.

She ran out along the road and nearly got run over by a car.

"Susan, good gracious!" said the driver. It was old Mr Grandly's fly-about grand-daughter who always came over Mondays to see to him. "Whatever's the matter? Here, calm yourself down. Sit still."

"It's Horse. They're going to plant Christmas trees all over Horse."

"They can't do that."

"They can. They can. It's because he's fading out, that's what it is."

She shook off the kind arm of the fly-about grand-daughter and ran on.

"Mother," she shrieked, flying into Sandy Top.

"Yes?" said her mother coming through the back door as if she had been down the slope to the village, which she had.

"They're going to dig up Horse. There's men bringing drain pipes and others bringing diggers, and others bringing thousands of Christmas trees."

"I know," said her mother. "I've just heard. I went down with your father to see what it's all about."

"I shall *die* if they plant trees all over Horse."

"No you won't," said her mother. "No sense in dying. We must do something though. Have your tea and do your homework while we think on."

"I *couldn't* do my homework. Mrs. Pail didn't even *give* us any homework. She's all of a flurry and Mr. Grandly has shut his door."

"Oh dear," said Susan's mother.

"And young Mr. Grandly doesn't care. He justs sits staring and the Shop do nothing but laugh and I haven't even told them. . ."

"What we've a need of is that fly-about grand-daughter."

"She's come. I saw her. But she'll be no good. She doesn't live here any more. Only Mondays and holidays. She doesn't care about Horse. Nobody cares about Horse."

"Sit to your tea and be quiet," said her father, coming in. "You're as crazed as old Grandly. He's saying it'll be the start of another war. Stop fretting. There's great goings on, so settle down."

"What's happened? What goings-on?"

"The forestry. They've tried taking the drain pipes up Sandy Back and they're stuck in the zig-zag."

"Stuck?"

"Aye—the whole contraption.

Stuck in the lane. It'll take armies to shift them. There's truck one side of a bend and drain pipes jack-knifed round the corner."

"Oh wonderful," said Susan, and then, "but oh the diggers! The diggers are coming tomorrow."

"That they're not," said her father. "They'll not get past the drain pipes."

"But they'll come round this way. Round the road and up here to Sandy Top and over. All the diggers. Then the trees."

"That they won't," said Susan's father. "Not over my private land. I tell you Susan, sit to your tea and then go to bed."

Chapter 4

The next day Susan woke with a heavy feeling and wondered why. Then she remembered.

She ate her breakfast early and went to school the long way round. She got to the village and crossed the square without even looking up at Horse, or what there was of him. She couldn't bear to.

Everyone was rather quiet and muttery. Across at the pub Mr. Grandly's door was still shut.

At play-time every one asked Mrs. Pail if they could go and look at the drain pipes stuck in the lane but she said no in case they got loose and came rolling down and squashed them all, causing more nuisance still.

There seemed very little to do in the square except make sandal patterns with the big pool of oil the artic-lorry had left behind on the stones.

Then the fly-about grand-daughter came hurtling from the front door of her arty holiday cottage with the gig lamps, looking very business-like and carrying over her arm a clean shirt. She disappeared in to the pub and there were the usual roaring noises as old Mr. Grandly was seen to. “That’s better,” she called to everyone, coming out again. “I think we’re about ready to start.”

A car or two and some people had appeared in the square. Susan’s parents were two of the people and the vicar was another and the fly-about grand-daughter greeted them. Then a land-rover drew up with an important farmer from over Thirsk in it, and then the vet and then the doctor and a few more, and they all went in to old Mr. Grandly's.

After a few minutes two more people came round the corner. The Shop's assistant and young Mr. Grandly. The Shop's assistant, who was also known as Silly Betty was sent over to the children and young Mr. Grandly straightened himself up, coughed twice, thrust out his chin and walked over Mr. Grandly's door step. It was the first time for many years.

Silly Betty came over and clapped her hands like a floppy seal and said, "Now then children, I'm looking after you today. In you go!" But nobody went in. They played tig and giggled and pushed each other and ran circles round Silly Betty and one or two (not Susan) even ran up on to Horse.

But after not very long at all Mrs. Pail came sweeping out of the pub and shooed off Silly Betty and said, "All's fixed. Come along now. It's Nature," and took the whole school in a neat crocodile with trowels and forks in a basket from under her teacher's desk; and they set to for the whole afternoon, clearing dandelions, scratching and digging out bushes and tussocks and ling and even precious bilberries.

When they had huge piles of these they stacked them up in the midst of Horse and set fire to them.

"But it'll spoil Horse more," said Susan.

"Rubbish," said Mrs. Pail. "He has

fire in his belly. Like the Bible. And so have we."

Smoke from the fire of the belly of Horse rose up to the late summer sky and people in the far-off trains across the Wolds looked out of the windows and said, "Look, they're burning stubble over on the Hartington Hills. There was once one of those White Horses set out over there. I wonder what happened to it?"

Chapter 5

The children were kept after school. The parents began to come to join them in ones and twos as the day drew on. More and more weeds and bushes and dandelions were piled on to Horse. From Horse's tail someone combed out a poor twisted leathery fox, dead two winters in a thistle patch. Slowly the little children grew tired and got taken home, but the older ones worked on—with trips for coke and biscuits to the Shop—until the moon came out. Then they began to get tired too and straggled off. At last even Susan began to get tired and was taken home by her mother up to the top and over, though her father stayed on. As Susan looked down back over the slope under the big September harvest moon she could see her father and Mrs. Pail and the important farmer and the vicar and the vet and the fly-about grand-daughter. Young Mr. Grandly was cutting a new, sweeping curve to Horse's flowing mane. Even Silly Betty was bending and toiling still, and old Mr. Grandly stood stately by the stile.

In the night she woke once and

found the huge clear-cut moon shining in through her window and she thought she heard lorries and shouting.

Oh, they've come, they've come, she thought, they've come to dig Horse up even so.

But she was tired and very achy and she fell asleep again.

She woke to a silent house.

She went downstairs and there were last night's dishes about and chairs all anyhow, which was not her mother's way. "Hello?" she called—but no answer. The clock ticked slowly and loudly and said it was nearly school-time.

"Oh gracious!" she said and

gathered up a piece of bread and ran like mad up to the top.

But the road at the top was blocked by three empty lorries with white insides and white spilling all down them and on to the ground. For a minute Susan thought, goodness, snow! Then—still a bit dozy and scared because of Mrs. Pail and the lateness—she careered down the hill again and round the bottom road, round the semi-circle, past the wood carver's where all was silent, past the

Shop where not a murmur and in to the village square.

Children were sitting about. Sitting everywhere—on the pub bench, on the window sills, on the rowan tree and Mrs. Pail with the school bell in her hand but not ringing it was standing out on the stones by the oil puddle—and old Mr. Grandly, magnificent in yesterday's clean shirt and a very ceremonial sort of a hat no one had ever seen before was on his doorstep in front of his open door. And young Mr. Grandly stood beside him.

All eyes were on Horse—and so at once were Susan's.

Horse stood there gleaming and glittering on the bank side. His hoof was prettily lifted, his head was daintily dropped, his mane and his tail—with not a hint in it of dead foxes—flowed like silver sea across the green grass.

A little dark man with a clip board and papers and a brief-case was standing in the square looking worried. "I never was told of this," he said, "I never heard of anything like this."

"It's been there for centuries," said Mrs Pail.

"Come in and see the photographs," said young Mr. Grandly.

"It's not on the maps. Antiquities—ruins and that are marked on the maps."

"Horse is no ruin," said old Mr. Grandly.

"No he's not that," said the little man. "He looks as if he was finished yesterday."

He caught Susan's eye. "What do you say to this then?" he asked. (The girl had a queer look as if she might be thinking about laughing and crying at the same time.) "What do you know about this horse?"

"He's always been there," said Susan, "as long as I can ever remember."

When the man had gone away to write a report and telephone people and ask for the Christmas trees to be sent somewhere else, Mrs. Pail herded them all in towards school and proper writing work. "An essay on fir trees," she said. "How they ought to fit the landscape, how they breed flies and you can't walk in them, how they drop needles and stop things growing more than any Horse, how you never hear a bird sing in them and how they look best cut down and decorated up for Christmas. Just a few ideas," she said, "and then we'll write another story about the lovely trees to be found in hedges and along our roadsides in the Wolds!"

As they went in from the square the three snowy lorries whizzed along the lower road. They were marked DANGER LIME with the name of the chemical firm where the fly-about grand-daughter's husband worked.

"Is it lime as in lime juice?" Susan asked Mr. Grandly, hanging back.

"That it's not."

"Is it like in limestone?"

"That it may be."

"Will Horse mind being limed over?"

"That he won't. Make him clean and sweet. And a good sharp shape."

"There may be some trouble," said the fly-about grand-daughter getting in to her car. "I'm away now, Grandfather. Keep fairly quiet."

"I'm away too," said young Mr. Grandly and shook hands with his father.

Susan and old Mr. Grandly were left alone in the square.

"Lot of fuss and hustle," said the old man.

"Aren't you glad we fussed and hustled?" said Susan.

"Well, I dare say."

"Well there then."

"Bairns has their uses. When their minds is off attachments."

He went very slowly through his old door, leaving it open. "Round the bottom road now tonight," he said, looking back. "We want no frosted feet. We forget all this now. We leave yon Horse to settle."

Susan ran over to school and looked up once more at Horse before she went in.

He sparkled in the sun. He shone. He seemed to dip his head at her.

And Susan waved.